THRICE PUBLISHING NFP, a private corporation
registered in the state of Illinois, reaches outside
the mainstream to publish the work of selected writers
whose efforts, we feel, need to be seen.
It's flagship publication, **THRICE FICTION**, has
been a platform for presenting this work alongside
exceptional artwork since 2011. **THRICE ARTS** provides
design and editing services to writers at large.

Volume 2 • Issue No. 2 • DECEMBER 2021
RW Spryszak, Editor
David Simmer II, Art Director

CONTENTS

Thrice Notes

I'm having trouble starting this. I have kudos to hand out, complaints to make, suggestions to offer, jokes to tell, but sometimes I feel as though I am only spitting into the wind. We, as writers who mostly live in the small press universe, are very good at offering moral support, "likes," "Congrats," and all that. But when it comes to supporting one another we fail, and pretty miserably sometimes. I don't know. It isn't a question of "schools" or "isms." One would hope that here in the 21st Century we don't need to be identified as being one theory or another (do we?). Having a manifesto anymore is just another form of mutual masturbation. And people get so snobby once they have an artistic or literary code to follow.

I once had the idea of starting a group that went out and bought each other's work in a continual round robin. You get a book published - I buy it. He gets an article in a magazine - she gets a short story in a prestigious, front tier litmag - I go out and buy a copy, or order a copy, or something. I got zero responses, except for the snotty looks of people who thought that kind of thing beneath their royal dignity or something. So I took it down and practice it on my own. I have more books by small publishers done by people I know in real life or fake life than a lot of people. All done in support, because I know one thing - there are excellent, innovative, solid writers who deserve more avenues, opportunities, recognition, and support than they get in the small circle jerk the Indies sometimes feel like. Who knows why they are not seen, or heard, or read.

James Claffey, our featured writer in this issue, is just exactly one of those people. We published his book "The Heart Crossways," a tour de force, a couple of years ago. And it's still as good as it was when it came out - just sayin'. Not that I'm trying to guilt you into getting a copy. I'm really not. I think - if you haven't read it (you can get it on Amazon, for the lazy among you) you are missing something. And if this issue of the magazine can showcase the range, style, and force of Claffey's work to you, and it intrigues you enough… well…what are you waiting for? I'm not going to send you a copy. You'll just have to do it on your own. You know, support each other?

•

Elsewhere in this issue we are honored, nay thrilled, to have Claire Rudy Foster give forth on the issue of writing trans characters into your work. I, for one, wanted to know how to address the issue in support, and asked for the article. Dig - it is presented here by someone who ought to know. So pay attention.

•

In the first issue of our second volume I suggested people write in for any reason and we'll publish what you have to say in a great big letters section. Start a discussion in letters. Arguments. Issues. Nah… never mind. Even the crickets were silent. So skip that idea too.

One thing for certain is that we shouldn't be able to blame the goddamned pandemic for not being productive. Those write best who write alone, (that's like my other favorite one - you know, "write high, edit sober") so there should be no excuse.

So that's enough from grouchy old RW for now. Don't smart me. 🌏

RW Spryszak

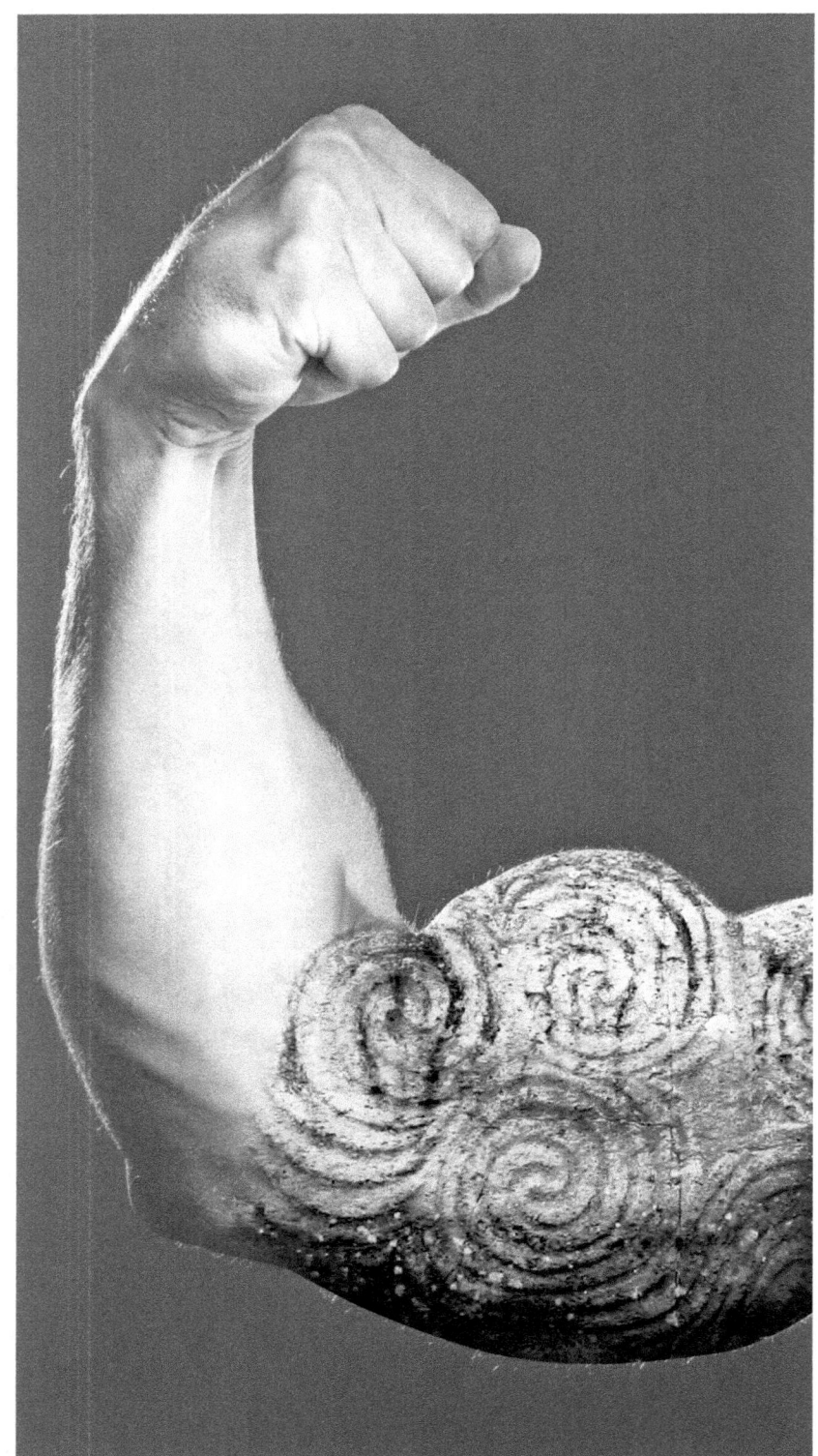

James Claffey

At Night

The anarchist in my closet comes out at night to feast on the remains of yesterday's dinner. His biceps are inked with Celtic spirals and his nipples circled by bronze. In the moonlit bedroom I sneak a look at him through my half-open eyelashes. He is familiar, having once stood guard over the crib when I tossed and turned, sick with the scarlet fever that took the neighbor's daughter. The sweat on his shoulder-blades glistens as he slips out to the living room, and the rustle of rats in the underbrush outside the window doesn't distract him.

Unstoppable as the Sea

Sky across cathedral roofs, the breeze shifting the white-and-yellow pennants, the gargoyles' downcast faces focused on the passers-by far below. Broken nose, chipped ear, the wounds of errant seabirds, their clumsy beaks pecking away at granite, unforgiving and long-lived. Under the bell, the clapper in his hand, he engineers the three o'clock chimes. His cassock billows, the white collar a makeshift bib. In his head he counts off the clicks of the cogs, an arithmetical task grown as old as the scar on his knee, a reminder of childhood mischief. His face, resolute and serious, betrays the scabs and lines of too many unheard prayers. Long ago from his deaf mother he learned the glory of bending with the wind, letting himself be carried along, unstoppable as the sea.

Unbutton

Love is a flood of moon captured on the nape of a bat's neck as it swallows and swings across the tops of the apple trees on a clear night in October. These are the fallow times before the sky fills with rain, the cart-ruts with mud, and the great copper vats with the golden cider we shall drink in the quiet corner of the green barn when you return from the city. I miss how we used to horse around in the dry straw, the silver flecks in your hair, the twin dimples when you smiled. Will you be whole when you return, or will time have taken from you the ability to unbutton and uncover the map of your skin; the contour lines and the elevations, the serried ridges of ribcage, the plowed field of your furrowed brow?

Three Sheets

On the corner of Capel Street a makeshift orchestra composed of violin, cello and harpist, play a Strauss waltz and an old couple turns circles in the rain. I envy them the carefree ability to let loose and give vent to their desires. I'm no rebel, given instead to reticence and silence. As I distance myself from the musicians the strains of their tune weave their way between the falling rain drops and find shelter in the doorway of McQuillan's Tool Shop.

At the Hugh Lane Gallery

Bonnard's *Boulevard de Clichy*. You with the paisley scarf and mitts, me gnawing my lip incessantly, until the skin comes away and the blood runs down my chin. You ask whether I am moved by the art, or am I nervous at the thought of your hands roaming my naked body in the cabin in the woods you're care-taking? I palm a warm chestnut from hand to hand and consider the street vendors frozen in canvas.

Lost Saint on Quiet Water

The boat cuts through the dark water leaving a churned whitish wake that stretches out towards the shore. After an hour or so, my hands hurt, red welts on the palms, spasming muscles in the small of my back. Even this far out there are reeds in the lake; long, wavering strands of lush green. The surface ripples and only the lowing of some far-off cattle in a field breaks the rolling movement of the water. I let the oars go and they rattle in the oarlocks whilst I lie back in the well of the boat. Above, the early evening stars impinge on the empty sky and I imagine the heavens to be a place of some certainty. Ashore, my family assembles for dinner, my place empty, and the questions. I sit up to look over the edge of the boat. Floating in the reeds is my grandmother's body, narrow and porous, a lost saint on a stretch of quiet water.

A Juggling Motion

My father sat at the end of my bed, tossing the skull from palm to palm, his shaking hands casting bird shadows on the bedroom wall. In the furrows of his thick-jointed fingers I could see the dark rich soil of his graveyard home, and the five geese that flew west this morning across the leafless sycamore trees, each of the birds calling out to the other as they crossed the silent soccer pitch below. He alighted too soon, bound for his cursed home beneath the wet wooden plank.

Geisha

We are putting on a play in class, and some of the boys are playing the female roles. Teacher says I am a tree. I don't know what a tree does, except it moves from side to side and makes whooshing sounds when the wind blows. Michael Murray got the main part as the Samurai lord because his mammy works for the parish priest, cooking his dinner and darning the holes in his gloves and socks caused by the stigmata. Daniel Lamb will play the main female because he has long blond hair and the teacher calls him a "Nancy boy." On the night of the performance, seven of us sway from side to side as Michael Murray pecks Daniel Lamb on the cheek and the audience goes, "Ooh."

No Confetti Wedding

Beastly drunk and off to golf, bushes lining the fairways as tangy cocktails. Judges in wigs passed down sentences on failed businesses, the festering sores of regret unhealed. When he drank, the saliva dried up and the white crust built about his lips as each swallow made a sad summer. Home waited, the mother cleaning the crystal decanters of smudged fingerprints.

Some Kind of Prize

The bonding between the older priest and he, a violin student, was awkward at first, but the way the man understood the boy's struggles, particularly the bad relationship with his dad; well, that was the one thing that pushed him over the edge. The strolls began innocently, along the bridle path that ran through the grounds of the seminary, and he loved how the priest named the various mushrooms and funguses that sprang up in the low grass. He believed the man saw him as some kind of prize; a teenager with greasy hair and a flick-knife comb that seemed cool. He loved that the previous Sunday the man had delivered the wafer to his mouth at communion and he had licked the jagged nail of the priestly thumb. Nobody saw, though his mother sat close to the altar, her eyes fixed on the tabernacle door, as if expecting Jesus himself to appear from the marble tomb.

Fissures

There's a spot at the base of your neck where a small transparent circle of flesh lives. When I ask you about this you say nothing. Instead, you scratch your scalp, look down at your feet, and mumble an excuse about wanting to get away for a bit. After a lunch of grilled root vegetables; fennel root, turnips, and musty purple potatoes, you let slip the news of a round-trip airfare sale on JetBlue. For a few weeks. To the islands. Time to think. Paper-chains of forgotten paradoxes, index-cards with abandoned recipes, the yellow notebook I gave you for your birthday. These are to be your comforts out there in the Far Tortuga's. I try to recall when exactly the perfect shape of our relationship began to show those narrow cracks, the fissures we opened by allowing our angry words to seep in. I accused you of being a dog with a bone. See how your beautiful snout worked its way into the opening and ruined our symmetry?

The Crack in my Heart

There is an accident bell that rings on the hour, bringing anguished screams from next-door's parrot. In the bedroom, between worn sheets with torn holes, the pair of us trade places in the deep hollowed mattress. She has a scar where they took the kidney for her sister's transplant, a purple knot of surgeon's haste. We have rhythm; in the way I fork lentils into her dropped lip, how she scratches her left temple with jagged fingernails. The earth, the energy, the thumping of waves on rock, how she breached the waves and plunged towards the fairytale waiting on the sandy floor. I failed to protect her and waded in wearing only a pair of Thorlo running socks and a half-off wetsuit. Now, she curls like a bean in the bed, her toes twiglike, the crown of youth long tumbled. Still, we endure. I am a bargain, a stay-at-home caretaker with less energy than a long-buried battery. When she is asleep I sometimes sneak into the garden and rearrange the sand dollars on the deck, souvenirs of early love. These days they form patterns I cannot decipher because of the lump in my throat and the crack in my heart.

The Sweetness of the Practiced Stroke

The swing creaks to-and-fro in the fog, the absence of a child telling everything except the why. How the seat curves in the middle despite the lack of weight to create the bow. Once, a swarm of bees terrorized the neighborhood, and the old man in number 7 took at them with an old Fred Perry Autograph tennis racket, dispatching dozens of still buzzing victims to the gravel. Maybe the ringleaders of the hive breakout zipped away from the playground in protective formation, or maybe the wallop of catgut caught them amidships and sent them to their gray doom. He was handy with the racket, even in his eighties, stone-deaf and unable to hear the sweetness of the practiced stroke as he cleaved the air. Later, after the last dog walkers quit the small park, he might have had a dollop of honey in his black tea to cut the edge of the tinnitus and to give balm to his memories of better days on neatly rolled grass courts at a private school now replaced by an automobile showroom.

Carved into Old Flesh

The surgeon's hands are tanned and hairless. He pulls on the latex gloves and calls for his conductor's baton. The shine of the blade in the harsh light of the theater dazzles, as he carves into old flesh. I remembered not having written the check for the registrar. Never mind. Time for all that later when she's in recovery. I catch my reflection in the stainless steel light shade. My eyes are too dark, like wet tea bags, and the beard is as thick and wiry as a badger's pelt. My hair hangs below my chin in two shiny tributaries. In years to come I will be painted by some stained-glass artist as a study for a window in some distant college campus in Idaho. I hold my breath as the surgeon exposes the papery object that was my mother's heart. It moves as if a lizard's belly is exposed to an idle boy's gaze and the machine putters and flat-lines as the surgeon raises both hands Christ-like in supplication, or defeat. I peer from behind his shoulder and blow a hot breath toward the still heart in his hands. Life anew. Rebirth.

Dearly Departed

The porridge oats soaked overnight in the double broiler and sat on top of the cold Aga range. Before turning the light off the woman took a moment to consider the St. Brigid's Cross on the wall and say a silent prayer for all in the house. At 6am came the rattle of glass from the Premier Dairies' milkman, who left full bottles of milk on the doorstep, foil tops covering a thick layer of cream. She had been dreaming of a crowded street and her small daughter who'd slipped her hand and got lost in the throng of shoppers. With the range lit and the porridge warming up she put a match to the first cigarette of the day. After holding the smoke in for a full half minute she remembered the dream. Realizing her daughter had actually been stillborn, the smoke rushed from her lungs, through her nostrils, mixing with the tears that rolled down her face.

The Prospect of Being Eaten

I began to squirrel away the rotten fruit the day I heard about the sea creature. We were living close to the ocean in a tall, narrow house with uneven stairs and slanted ceilings. This was the year my voice broke, my fourteenth. Mornings, I walked the dog along the pebbly beach, the mist everywhere. I'd gone into the small local shop to buy some scraps for the dog. One of the old fellows was buying a quart of whiskey, already peeling the brown bag away from the neck of the bottle, when he said to the shopkeeper, "Lives down the swampy end of town. Grotesque. Swear its two eyes travel in different directions." The shopkeeper dismissed the codger's tale and returned to his dusting. I paid for the scraps, took off for home, determined to see this creature of which the man had spoken. Wrapped in my Eskimo anorak, I had an uneasy feeling as I crunched over the beach towards the marshy part of the estuary. What if this beast had rotten teeth and jagged claws?

The smell was what caught my attention first. A strange odor, almost a fizziness that attached itself to the teeth: death. How I wished I'd taken a swig of my mother's "medicinal" brandy on the way out the door. Instead, my feet cold in my boots—the socks wet through—I clambered over a giant piece of driftwood and scanned the area. Nothing. As I turned to go, a low, guttural rasp called across the water. I could make out a slender shape near the shoreline, an oily drum-like mass, two penetrating eyes, yellow wandering irises. My backside itched, and the prospect of being eaten turning me to jelly. The thing sucked and slobbered its way towards me and all I could do was follow the misleading direction of its gaze as the last few steps grew close and my bowels loosened.

A Chalice from Viking Times

My father bought dozens of pairs of Wellington boots made from India rubber. "Caoutchouc," he said, tweaking my ear. "Collected in the tropics by slaves of the Empire and sold here by Yours Truly." His mustache tickled my cheek as he kissed me. A man of habits. A man of rules. "Always pepper and salt your food," he said. I remember how he'd mop up the oil from the sardine can with his bread and smack his lips in delight. He never ordered less than two drinks at a time, as he believed, "The devil makes work for idle hands." As a lad in school, according to my mother, he had a strange look to him, almost as if he'd wandered off the Silk Road and into the wide-open brown expanse of the Bog of Allen. Once, they found a chalice from Viking times, and the skeleton of a woman who read tea leaves outside a ruined oratory on the Clara Road. When he wasn't looking, I'd take the leather case with embossed red serge flowers and stare at him in the photo. I missed him when he went away. My mother said a jury of his peers had undone him, though, at the time, I'd no idea what she meant. All I knew was she met with the local politician in the conference room of the family business and when she emerged she was wiping her mouth on her sleeve. A month later my father was delivered back to us from his cell in Portlaoise Prison.

A Dish Best Served Unnoticed

Traipsing about the city under threat of rain, amazing thunderheads rolling over the Dublin Mountains, the thick accumulation of gray a thumbed smudge print on a child's exercise book. I had pulled myself together since you'd left, my pride swallowed, I'd begun meetings in the Protestant hall—"Getting to Grips with Your Anger"—and had even shared several of the embarrassing tales of your mistreatment. It never struck me that you were the one needing help, consumed as I was by a love in blinders. That time you slapped me on the side of the head with the stapler: blurred vision and three stitches. The other time you twisted my arm behind my back and wrecked my shoulder.

My friends all said I'd be better off leaving you, though I thought differently, dogged bastard that I am. There was a moment when I expected you to murder me in my sleep. A zip file of each of the times you beat me, or threatened me, or pretended to, is hidden in my office at work—just in case. Your taste in clothes kept me chained to the dog post of your love. Those diaphanous and tormenting patterned dresses acted like a narcotic, and I refused to accept the obvious truths inscribed on my bruised torso. In the cool afternoons when you were away ocean swimming I prayed to the Virgin Mary and the Christ Child for a sneaker wave of revenge to suck you below and fill your breathless lungs with water.

In Search of a Safe Haven

Ship in a bottle, rolling about on plastic seas, the waves eternal, the wind currents caught in a forever updraft. Old hands twiddle and fidget with the fragile lumber, the magnifying glass as large as a dinner plate, allowing him to place each spar and strut exactly where it needs to go. Under the table clumped hair in puffballs rolls soft in the evening air, and from outside, the rising call of a downy woodpecker trills. One slip, the glue semi-set, and the netting crushed between shaky fingers, sets him off.

On the back steps he scans the trees for a sight of the bird, but the low sun in his eyes makes it hard to pinpoint where it perches. The long trill again and this time he thinks he spies a black-and-white blur on the low branch of an elm tree. Again the call, again a flash of white throat. "Shut up, shut up, shut up!" he yells into the garden.

In mockery the bird makes its call again. He hefts the bottle in his hand, fingers tracing the raised letters, and lets it fly in a wobbling arc towards the tree. The glass explodes and a cloud of disconnected leaves flutters to the ground. One hand on the water heater roof, he wheezes in short breaths as the woodpecker flashes through the orchard in search of a safe haven.

Apparition of the BVM

The hose was used to suffocate the parish priest. That's the way my grandfather told the story the night of the big wind. He drank steadily from noon to midnight perched at the bar. My grandmother reared her fifteen children without so much as a by your leave. He was besotted with Tullamore Dew, a lifelong love affair that ended in the sanatorium at Grangegorman. Three previous spells in St. John of Gods did him no good. Anyway, to tell it straight, he was surrounded by a cluster of his buddies, glasses piled all along the bar, his laugh ricocheting off the walls, and the tale of the priest's death laid out as straight as the poor cleric's body the day of the wake. My grandfather coughed explosively and was banging his fists against the counter, saying that the autopsy by the State's pathologist, Dr. Harbison had been a sham and a cover-up due to there being a young girl involved with the priest that night. Supposedly, she was a schoolgirl from Portumna who'd witnessed the Blessed Virgin Mary appear in a TV Repair Shop window at Halloween a few years ago. The audience at the bar listened as if he were on stage in front of a fancy microphone, the tall tales dripping from his lips like rain from a gutter.

Motherlove

She carves the intricate letters across her thigh and staunches the flow of blood with a dirty bandage grabbed from the trunk of an old VW Bug with a case of terminal rust and the paper chain of old hamburger wrappers and dust graffiti on the windows where her neighborhood's boys and girls scrawled "wash me" and the turquoise bangle hidden in the wheel well where she'd dropped it one dark night as she searched for the car jack as the boy who she was driving home shuffled about at the side of the road directing the beam of flashlight on her and the unwashed socks from her soccer kit as stiff and crumpled as a kitten's corpse in an overgrown garden and the love song the cowboy sent her from the Angola Prison where he was doing nineteen to life for bashing his poor mother's head in with an iron skillet and his father blind and destitute in the courtroom the day his son was sentenced and how she strums her guitar some nights and sings his sad love into the dried undergrowth at the back of her trailer where she hides her stash in an old coffee can beneath a pile of chopped wood where the black widows plot revenge against the world and the faraway look in her eyes as she tells of the teacher who used sneak her Snicker bars to stave off painful starvation and the way her eyes welled with tears as she told him she was okay and to give her some room because she couldn't breathe and the minute she got home she'd have to attend to her mother passed out drunk on the kitchen floor.

My City

This is my city, the one with the iron railings and the narrow lanes, the red-bricked houses and the slated roofs, the one with the green post boxes that used to be red, Rule Britannia, and the one with the statues facing inwards so as to reserve justice only for the rulers. My city, with its gardens of rhododendrons and monkey puzzle trees, gardens of carnations and roses and hydrangeas, and wasps' nests stuck in the corners of rickety garden sheds. My city, where I lied and stole and cheated my way through adolescence, where I kissed a girl for the first time and waited years before doing it again. My city, where I pedaled my bicycle through puddles and rainstorms, past closed shops at midnight, through deserted parks where mallards slept in groups for safety. My city, where I was singled out and labeled from early on, condemned me to follow some prescribed path chosen by the rule-makers. My city, where I struggled to find my true voice; once at nineteen reading a terrible imitation of a fantasy novel to a group of friends in a nondescript coffee shop. My city, where I watched the world go by without me, where the entire population upped sticks and hoofed it to the Phoenix Park to see the Pope, and I stayed home with my invalid father, more concerned he might die while we were out than I was at seeing the head of the Holy Roman Church. My city, of slow-running streams and horse chestnut trees, of canal locks and murdered swans. My city of writers, whose names are as recognized as the rain clouds that gather over the Dublin Mountains, whose skin I shed long ago, but whose bricks and mortar and smoky pubs and sharp-tongued humor make up the better part of me. Tonight, I miss my city and the house I grew up in, now inhabited by others, and my own mother unsure of everything, but safe in the care of nursing home staff in the new world she inhabits and in which she will surely die. *Oh, clement. Oh, loving.* Streets of cobbled stones and grated cellars where the barrels of porter and beer disappear and the stories are told to listeners eager for a wise word and a good laugh.

This Writer's Life—Imagined

Uncashed checks sit on the desk amidst your printed out stories and the neon Post-Its with lists for everything on them. That bottle of Oban your agent sent on publication of your novel is completely drained, the congratulatory note in silver Sharpie still readable on the glass. Playing card hearts and gambling chips mix with severed doll heads and linen handkerchiefs. Yours is a life complicated by more than the bad habits that bring excess weight to your frame daily. When you look in the mirror the fleshy jowls of your dead father take form, and the hairline you monitor assiduously darkens with hair-oil. You pop a painkiller and wash it down with the Tullamore Dew your brother sent for Christmas. He knows you only like Jameson's, but he's never been one to pander. A painting by your wife tilts towards the ocean, the figure unrecognizable, the colors a dust storm of nasty cranberry and lime. Your paperclip, the one you clean your ears with, crusted and minging, is beside the broken paperweight. Projects you start and make vague signs of finishing are all over the floor. Novel. Novella. Collection of stories. Failed myths from a one-sided love affair of long ago. The fedora you bought in New Orleans sits on your bust of James Joyce, hiding his blind stare. These days you are forgetful, always arguing on the phone with whoever will listen. The padded ring of fat about your waist reminds you of all that has gone before. Maybe you'll light a match and fire the candle on the mantel, summon the spirit of your dead father to berate him for not spending enough "quality time" with you when you were a boy. Regrets are festering, their dogged claws deep into your scalp. Give up the moody brooding, give up the slack-jawed looks you cast towards the mountains.

Murder—My Legacy

Gloves of otter skin and a fur-lined anorak, dressed for the arrayal. The brittle leaves were destroyed underfoot as the dead bird rattled in the cardboard box. Children's hearts are empty when it comes to knowing deep grief, or at least they are up to a certain age. There had been no visible signs of struggle. The hen appeared quite normal when I collected the eggs that morning. Certainly, she was loud, her ire expressed with a piercing cry at seeing her treasure pilfered. The hole we dug was ample for the shoebox, the soil dark and moist like wet coffee grounds, a small pool of water in the bottom of the grave. Looking back, I thought the creature's breast was swollen, abnormally so, perhaps some cardiac condition known only to poultry. Anyway, we dug the hole smack-dab in the middle of my mother's manicured lawn. My parents were out of town on a weekend "getaway," and I was the man of the house. Murder. My legacy. After the box was in the ground, we dumped the soil on top and patted it down tightly in case the bird came back to life and haunted us. When we finished, I thumped my best friend on the back and headed towards the house as the slanted sun poured its bloody light on the fresh earthen mound.

The Sky Suffocated

Cornered. The sky suffocated bore down oppressive. In the night the rain made gentle, the flood still far off, and downstairs on the dining-room table the centerpiece collected dust as the hours passed. The previous night we'd eaten a feast of Manchego cheese and bloody Rioja, our laughter rippling off the room's bare walls. We'd all dressed in Elizabethan garb, stiff collars and tight knickerbockers, the ladies in velvet gowns with tight-tied stays. As we caroused to the baroque music on the radiogram, our neighbor showed up carrying a frilled lizard with bloodshot eyes and proceeded to roar at us about the "Damned hurdy-gurdy music" giving his poor pet anxiety. I was too drunk to muster up a decent reply, my mouth forming the words I couldn't deliver. Instead, I waved my napkin in concession and went over to the radiogram and killed the switch. The neighbor departed with his live baggage under his arm, and we continued to drink the Rioja, this time humming soft music under our breath.

A Dollop of Love

A gas meter by the hall door was raided on those weeks he didn't bring home enough money to keep the lights on and the gas burning. Shame, a constant bedfellow; nights ran on a timetable as rigid as the trains out of Heuston Station. At 6:30 the news ended and the weather decreed, my ma would click off the old Ferguson television and produce the Rosary beads. Pale mother-of-pearl, handed down by her mother who'd had them brought back blessed at Lourdes. In line we'd face the wall, kneeling in front of my aunt's unfinished pastels of swans in reeds by some unnamed lake. The prayers dropped from our lips, thick as a swarm of bees about the pollen-heavy flowers in the back garden.

> *Joyful.*
> *Sorrowful.*
> *Glorious.*
> *Luminous.*

Mysteries of the scourging of the Lord, his bare flesh rent by lead-tipped flail. Mary Magdalene might've given him a dollop of love for the terrible pain. 'There," my father remarked, "was a woman, a barefaced hussy, forgiven for her sins by a better man than I, Gunga Din," he'd say. And should failed prayers have dropped from my lips, he'd turn the color of medium-rare steak and sputter curses, his thumb and forefinger rubbing the beads raw. The blame for our heathen ways was laid squarely at our ma's feet, as she let me listen to pop music and the hurdy-gurdy screams of drug addicts and wasters. Val Doonican and Andy Williams were the High Priests of his musical church, and above them, sitting at the throne of Heaven were Count John McCormack and Percy French. More than once the Old Man blistered my arse to the tune of, "The Mountains of Mourne." Now that he's gone almost fifteen years, I'd give a great deal to hear him sing those plaintive lyrics once more, the sting of his hand on my skin as close an approximation of love as I ever knew. I swear this soft voice sometimes comes to me, whispering, "But for all these great powers he's wishful like me, to be back where the dark Mourne sweeps down to the sea."

Straight Roads & Gentle Swells

The still form of the fallen bird, feathers ruffled in place at the exact moment of death. The world is a private one, a container of secrets and shames, of reputations and damage done over years, of stark landscapes and icy skies. Paper treasures store memories like holdfasts on coastal rocks buffeted by storm waves and wild surf. The toast was to a new year of straight roads and gentle swells of pastureland as far as the eye can see. Home is a broken nose, the ridge offset and the shadow of damage contained in a crooked expression. No more to creep the streets, head bowed, shame a relentless badge of failed marriage and crushed spirits. The old clothes of last year are shed, the soil and insects already working the weave to return the material to compost. This time should be one where action is the better course to tread, the dead-end of inactivity and passive reply to a closed-off street. In the morning light the dead bird is still, yellow beak and feet cold and brittle. The nare contains blood, a speckle, perhaps a hawk's attack from above. Mothers recede in the dawn, their white hair thinner and washed gold spun in the lamplight. Change is the washrag with which I shall wipe away the sins of past days, the bitterest almonds stinking of deathlove and the peel of a thousand oranges decaying in the barrel. Maybe it is time to let the dog wag its tail instead of the other way round. Cheap brandy, fur-lined gloves and shorn fields, empty cabins and plump pillows are the watchwords for writer's tears and dropped phone calls from home. Alive and at sea, the sails billow with fresh winds from the West and towards those distant drumlins the small craft breaks the waves, her proud prow and oiled oar-locks renewed for the voyage ahead.

Polishing Fruit

We've had our Indian Summer, Johnson's Baby Oil in Stephen's Green at lunchtime, "Zenyatta Mondata," blasting through the CD Walkman. "Please don't stand so... so close to me." Anthem for a shabby youth. The bastard shutters of the shop are touchy and difficult to open. I hate when the rolled metal grille slams up into the awning and the collected rainwater drenches me. I hate this fucking job. Get the newspapers, cut the twine and set them all out—"Times, Indo, Press, Sun, Mail, Express, Guardian, Times, FT," and three "Cork Examiners," special order for local priests on "special assignment." If I have to polish the bloody fruit again, today, there'll be hell to pay. I am sick to my back teeth of shining the Granny Smiths and Red Delicious with Pledge furniture polish. It's a minor miracle someone hasn't come in complaining of food poisoning, or dead worms. Here they come now, the cheapest effers in the city, all looking for their cut-price smokes and the page-3 nudies. "Go on, give us the money, Missus. What's keeping you from getting it out of your purse?" Fumble-fingers. Too much to drink. She was in John of God's last month, on the cure. Thirty pence, "The Times." And your man with the tweed overcoat and trilby? Would you look at the legs on him; Shirley Fucking MacLaine. Done up all business-like from the waist up, and a hoor from the dockyards from the waist down. He's sporting a nice pair of shiny black stilettos this morning, nonetheless. More things under this heaven and earth, as the Ma says to me sometimes.

The Songbirds Sang Death

This morning the songbirds sang death from the sun-drenched leaves of the MacArthur avocado tree. Of whose death they sang, I do not know. All I do know is their song struck the somber notes of Gounod's *messe solennelle*. Today is the feast of the Immaculate Conception, and home in Ireland, the busiest shopping weekend of the year. The dim shadow of my past falls across the sunned boughs of the avocado tree. Days are filled with sound: students' voices, their constant hum, the tidal flow of one period into another as the bells go and the passing period begins. Nights consumed; grading, planning, stressing. The death-song of the warbler, perched above the feasting coyote whose teeth tear the soft flesh of the fallen fruit. Ahead, the year's end waits in silence, with patience, to the side of the stage. At the turn of the year the clocks shall fall silent. All the birds shall repair to brittle nests and windy perches, to sing life anew. Conceive. Immaculate. Sign of the Cross. We march, too, in step with the soundtrack in our heads, to war, to war, to the slow beat drum and the clear fife. This year, absence pays a heavier toll for some reason. I remember all the Christmases of childhood, the smells of the kitchen, the tinsel, holly boughs, shiny garlands, banked fires, and the tree littered with aged decorations from better times. Always, on the music-stand lamp table, the tiny white tree with felt snowmen and angels; the tree my mother brought to me the year I spent in hospital with nephritis for the holidays. This tree, too, is faded, fallen apart, and gone. Nothing more than a memory in the cluttered hive of my head. The memories withdraw, deeper and deeper into the shadows, the faint light like lost earrings on a sandy shore.

The Torn Fingers of the Afflicted

The Saint's eyes downcast, wooden bed frame collecting dust, the evidence of an unhappy marriage was contained in the untidy row of fingernail shards embedded in the pine headboard. Nights meant a stiff drink; whiskey for him, and for her a frilled cocktail with tropical fruit juice. When they'd first met there'd been gentleness, and long walks on the heath. Now, if she so much as folded a napkin the wrong way, or licked the peanut butter for the kids' lunches off her fingers, he'd roar, his mouth the blaring train tunnel of rage. She'd known about his baggage before their first date, the name of his ex-wife, her prominent face on the bus benches about town, selling real estate—"A Name You Can Count On." She dreamed, unsettling dreams of him using his ex-wife's body as a fleshy abacus, his fingers greedily running along her ribs, the satisfied moans from the adding machine underneath. Flooded, was how the therapist put it, the way his emotions welled up like a spring tide, and overflowing the berm of marriage, filled with nasty words and even nastier blows, all disguised by long-sleeved garments and the careful application of make-up. For birthdays and holidays he made sure she painted her nails and edged her fear with several drinks. She, for her own comfort, palmed several Xanax and allowed the pillowy distance between them to inoculate her from his barrage of criticism. So it was that under the portrait of Saint Martin de Porres, she choked back her tears and dug her fingers into the wood as Chopin soothed the pain and her husband bore beastly down, condemned as he was by the judgment of the watching *almoner*, his blurry face dropping tears of sadness to soothe the torn fingers of the afflicted.

What Goes Unsaid

Say I hadn't gouged my arm on top of that wall and that you'd stayed asleep while we plundered the neighbor's apple trees? Say the sun had been shining that day instead of clouds and rooftops commingling in a uniformity of slate gray? Say I walked the beam of the rotting plank of wood all the way to the cemented crown of glass studded into the cement? Say I felt a ripple of pleasure as both my hands closed around a glossy red apple? Say you had turned up for that date you were supposed to have with the assistant bank manager on the 5th of September, 1958? Would things have been different, then? Would you have entered into a romantic affair with him and changed the course of your spinsterhood, forever? Would you have renewed your vows in the small chapel in Inchicore where years later I'd cycle past on my way to soccer training? Would you have been too busy being a good, dutiful wife baking breads and tarts and confections for a comfortably middle-class Protestant from Magherafelt? None of this came to pass, and instead you spent the best part of forty years mining earwax from dark channels, all the time reading trashy romance novels, sneaking nips of whiskey from the flask you concealed in your handbag. Instead, you brought home your own bacon, leaving no doubt as to your true intentions. Say the form of your spreading body sent the bathwater over the edge and down into the kitchen, where I scratched answers to mathematics questions on grid paper, my school tie unloose about my neck, the patter of rain on the window panes, and your drowning bulk at the bottom of the tub upstairs.

Sitting Shiva

Always on about catching a chill, making sure to wrap up well against the cold and rain. Mornings, cod liver oil on a spoon. The St. Brigid's cross beside the front door, tacked to the Holy Water font. The bit of sponge in the well of the font yellowed and crusted, never changed in the years we've lived in the house. This shrine to saints and sinners; from the statue of Our Lady in my bedroom, her arms benevolently spread to forgive my sins, to the unlabeled bottle of clear fluid in the bureau in the dining room: Poitín. Under the sensible underwear in my mother's dresser drawer, a starting pistol, in case of robbery. Sometimes we'd steal it and chase one another up and down stairs, like Starsky and Hutch on a mission. Always a biscuit tin in the press. Kimberley, Mikado, or Coconut Creams, but inside, the chocolate cake with sliced Glacé cherries circled about the top. Everywhere, the fingerprints of the dead, relatives' faces on laminated Mass cards, "Pray for the repose of the soul," or, "Dearly Beloved," and the thick stack of aunts, uncles, cousins, and distant relations secured by a large rubber band. Method of death went largely unreported, hushed conversations late at night, tut-tutting and shaking of heads. "He was a young man, in his prime, too."

Hoarse the pot mender's cries as the cart trundled up the tarmacadam road, the pulling nag with its unkempt mane and the fellow atop the cart with hat angled to keep the sun out of his eyes. Those days a swarm of young ones followed the horse and cart, its pied piper calling out for business. Regretful words from hoity-toity housewives, afraid to trust the stranger's craft. Be careful he doesn't touch your hand and send a blush withering through your innards. A neighborhood dog yelps at the palsied horse, but the creature simply lifts a hoof and shakes a head at a cloud of flies. On the floor of the sitting room paint-by-number books are spread open, crayons and markers littered about, whilst we press noses to the windowpanes and cower when the stranger looks our way. The bust of some ancient pope sits on the marble mantelpiece, guardian of our small world. When the rain falls heavy the garden floods and the dug beds turn into moats protecting the grass square in the middle. Panic if the water reaches the doorstop. A knitted, stuffed serpent keeps out the breeze, but mildew and time rot its insides cancerous and it disappears in the Sunday night dustbin ritual. The coal men heave sacks of black nuggets onto their wide and bowed backs and strain to deliver their loads into the shed beside the dormant rhododendrons. How the cigarette lit stays stuck to the lip as ninety pounds of coal tumbles into the open door. Magpies preen glossed feathers in the branches of next-door's apple tree, the pecking interrupted by the now-and-again chatter of their talk. When old Mr. Fagan dies of loneliness the polished hearse sails up the road and top-hatted men carry him out in a mahogany box. We light a candle in the window for the repose of his soul, and his house sits Shiva for many a year before a childless couple move in and mourn their own losses.

Lost at Sea

Every wave that crashes on the rocks sends particles of ancient dead souls to the sandy shore. Once, caught in a storm, the dog got swept off the pier. Maybe he went after the poor creature and ended up caught in a current from which he could not escape, his red hair like sinking seaweed. He played soccer with us in Ahaganish Park. No real memory beyond that, I have to admit. Where is he? Dead and buried beneath the Irish Sea. Swept away. Perished.

Beloved son of Timothy and Maura.

Mourned by a sister, Dervla, and loving brothers, Ronan and Brendan.

Perhaps it was mental illness because people simply didn't disappear like that. Not something they considered. Blissful. Silent water. He fell into the silvered sea. The lights of shore faded as the oxygen molecules dissipated. Not sure if he drowned, or was lost. Now can see—the coldest fish invigorated by the warmth of his submerged soul. His was a total immersion. Skylight to a distant opening. Love and how to pursue unseen creatures through the kelp beds. Sink. Beneath. Weight of falling bodies. Through water. Inimitable. We are shades of older visitors. In depths beyond our ability to function. He waved his arms once and fell through the space into a narrow opening. Not to be heard from again. Nameless. I'll sing a song, raise a glass to the Scobation boy. All those years ago. Thirty, maybe more. No more than the brain can imprint odd images on the granulated surface of a gelatin plate. Loved. He was loved by a family. Heart. Broken. Mother's tears. In the hallway the dog's leash collects dust.

Soldiers of Christ

I dreamt of having a turtle as a pet. Lampy Egan owned one, a slow moving little fellow with a chunk missing from the shell. Caught a blow from the coal shovel one night when Shane was filling the scuttle for the fire. We played French cricket in the laneway across from our house, the walls narrow as the passage tomb at Newgrange. I wasn't very good at bowling. The tennis ball didn't fit properly in my hand and I'd release it too soon. Larry or Donal Driscoll, the twins, tapped the head of the tennis racket on the ground so hard the echoes went on for minutes. Their old man was a bear with thick black hair all over his back and a head of wiry white hair on top. He'd take one look at you and melt the heart inside you with fear. Those lads sported bruises from Spy Wednesday to the Assumption of the Blessed Virgin. Once, we snuck into the plant hire yard and tipped the front bucket loaders out on the ground, sending floods of water rushing down the lane, saturating the gaff. I thought it was a great trick altogether, but when the security guard with the radio in his hand set the dog on us; well, it was a different story. Our bikes were in the lane on the other side of the gates, so we legged it for freedom, the Alsatian at our heels. Shane wanted no part of our mission, preferring to stay home and play checkers with his blind grandfather. When the turtle died we cut away the flesh from the shell and cleaned the insides with Brillo pads and stored our bangers in the hollow. A team, we were inseparable most of the time. Fridays we'd scour the racks of the newsagents for the weekly comics, always trying to steal the free gifts inside the issues, watching for the shop girl to go into the back for her tea break. Creatures of sin were we, Soldiers of Christ, trained by the Monsignor himself to ring the bell at the right time and bring him his afternoon post on the silver salver inside the front door of the parochial house. Sometimes he'd press a few bob into our hands, ruffle Shane's curly hair with those stodgy fingers he held the host in the air with at Mass. Once a year he'd have gashes on his hands, but we never thought to ask where they came from, for fear of finding out the truth.

Unfixable

Cannibalism was not on my mind as I sat with my mother's coffined body. I'd read the *Tibetan Book of the Dead* and of corpses that moved and how Holy men would attempt to capture the spirit of the dead by latching onto the body and waiting for the tongue to protrude from the mouth. Once this happened, they'd bite it off, and with it, the spirit of the person. I didn't read too closely the part that told of how the spirit turned into a whirling dervish and at times could take the lives of anyone close. I ignored that part, as I wanted to save my mother's soul too much.

At midnight on the eve of the burial, I closed the front door on the last visitor, a third cousin twice removed from Sheepshead Bay. When he was gone, I went into the parlor, climbed atop the pine coffin and wrapped my arms and legs about her stiffening body. The book said I'd have to cover her mouth with mine and the thought of it made me want to throw up, but the memories of her love and the shabby dresses she wore to church on Sundays; well, I had no choice, did I?

The cat downstairs was scratching the baseboards in search of mice and my mouth was glued to the mother's. I could feel her melt beneath me and begin to thrash about in the coffin, upsetting the candles lit on both ends. *Quit your wriggling*, I said, her eyes unfixable and moving from side to side in panic. If I weren't careful, she'd be the death of me. Her legs were flying at this point, the coffin rocking precipitously, her Rosary beads clicking time.

Astride her, my fear unbearable, I clustered her limbs together and pressed my lips even tighter. She tasted of Woodbine cigarettes and Eau de Cologne 4711. My childhood wove patterns in the air above the coffin as I waited for her mouth to part and her tongue to press between my own two lips. The spasming of her eyelid must have tipped me off to the moment, for just then, under the gaze of the Blessed Virgin's portrait, I felt the cold triangle of her flesh.

My heart thumped and I bit hard on her tongue, chewing vigorously until it came away in my mouth. All calmed in that moment. Her body reclined into the rich velvet of the lined box and whatever creature had come alive in her withdrew. Into a square of aluminum foil I wrapped the gray flesh of her tongue and slipped it behind the rainbow trout in the freezer drawer of the fridge.

When the undertaker's man screwed the lid down the next morning he didn't give her mouth a second glance. I washed my breakfast down with a mouthful of hot tea and slipped out the door to the waiting hearse. Some problems in life are unmapped and left to the explorers of the world to unearth. My mother's spirit lived now in me, the wedge of flesh safe and sound in the freezer, my worry of being abandoned in this life all but put to rest.

Threnody for the Living

She sits with the television set turned on, sound to mute. She likes it for the company. The moving pictures keep her from being alone. When I think of this existence, this lonely ritual, I imagine crawling into my mother's head and seeing life from her point of view. What an impossible task to set before a person. All the way back to the years before the Second World War, she could go to her hometown in the middle of Ireland, with its large cathedral and thriving marketplace.

The names of childhood friends and who owned what shop, and who drowned in the river that year the Shannon froze over are fresh in her mind. Ask her what she had for breakfast, or dinner yesterday, and she'll concoct a lie, an untruth, to cover the reality of aging. Memory allows her to put on an act wherein she can say, "Oh, we had a lovely roast chicken for dinner, and breakfast was toast and marmalade and soft-boiled eggs." There is a "One Way" sign imprinted in her mind, pointing to the hillside cemetery where her husband is fifteen years under the soil. Marking time, the metronome of days, each like a leaf falling from an autumn tree, she watches and waits.

Before she entered the nursing home she left raw chicken in a bowl on top of the heater beside the fridge. Weeks, it could have been festering. Meals on Wheels came and went, deposited on the doorstep the days she was out at medical appointments, placed in the fridge for safekeeping, never to be eaten. Towels in her bathroom mildewed from inactivity. She wore the same clothes day after day, laundry rarely done, dust and dirt thickening on the furniture. When I'd call her to check in, everything would be "Great! Sure, the weather's awful. And how are you?" Patterns. Closed cycles. The conversation was a skillfully written script we adhered to every Sunday, rarely making forays into areas where uncertainty dwelt.

I am practicing her rituals. When the house is quiet, our child in bed, wife at work, or out writing with a friend, I turn to Netflix on my laptop and mute the sound. Alone in my office I sit and stare at the screen, the words mouthed by unfamiliar mummers. I enter her body; feel the weariness of her eighty-five-year-old bones, the glaucoma-scarred eyes, and the fingers crooked with arthritis. I am her. She is I. Blood of my blood. Constructed from her DNA and that of my father. Shall I succumb to a stroke in old age like my father, or shall my brain become fogged by dementia and render me no longer able to operate on an even keel? Life is uncertain, and I struggle to comprehend its meaning and purpose. Meanwhile, she sits in front of the silent screen, watching her endgame play out to an untimed soundtrack.

Brú na Bóinne—July Afternoon

Spun wool whirls about the loom.

A merchant's daughter is named for the minstrel Goddess, Doon.

Slow-flowing water meanders around the ancient mound.

Soup of the Day is always vegetable soup.

The Americans pray over their lunch as the heathen Irish get to their food

straight away.

Late-Victorian graffiti marks the soft stone inside the passage.

Sign up for the solstice lottery.

St. Brigid's Crosses go for 7 a shot.

Inside the dark passage grave the walls are narrow

(The ancient Irish must have been rake-thin souls).

Rain buckets down all afternoon.

Spirals.

Spirals.

Spirals.

Cork—July Morning

Brook water fast flowing over mossy stones.
A dog more badger than canine saunters up the road.
Black-and-white Friesians head butt and chase one another.
It's Murphys, not Guinness in these woods.
A ruined church sits in high grass, windows bricked.
The busker covers the amp and guitar case with a shawl
as the pewter-colored rain clouds sing raindrops.
Salmon and hake stare wall-eyed from an icy bed.
The Turkish coffee seller makes thick lattes for 3.50.
Americans file noisily along the narrow footpaths in slickers.
To the South, Roche's Point lighthouse perches above the
crashing water.
A needle and thread discarded on a wet park bench.

Stephen's Green—False Summer 2018

A homeless man works two white swans like a snake charmer.
Tourists snap photos of the unfolding trauma.
The famine memorial is ignored by passers by and in a far cor-
ner a colorful
Oscar Wilde lies recumbent on a boulder.
Clouds whitefluffywisped march across the city sky.
Men and children in stocks mimic the poor souls of another
time.
Ducklings paddle about the slow Liffey water.
The orange wall has faded some since the last visit.
Arthur Guinness's statue watches over the main street of his
town.
A dead hedgehog lies in the wet grass.
In the Museum of Dead Animals the giant red elk are still ex-
tinct.
Disembodied bog people are fodder for Instagram.
My mother retreats along the corridor, back bent, wits awry.

Plucked Courage

The word was owl and the creature had lodged between the spotlight on the garage roof and the junction where the metal rod was affixed. Unmapped acres in every direction, the birds flew low patrols across the fields. The muttering of the homeless lady with the rollaway suitcases and terrible voice interrupted the quiet night. Her left eyelid drooped precariously, giving her the look of a broken doll, the long eyelashes over pools of aquamarine. Rescue was not in my mind as I cleared the scum off the water barrel out back, the last flicker of light fast disappearing as the moon hung back, abashed and afraid to rise. I could tell the bird was hurt from the thumping of its wing on tar paper. Plucked courage, I leaned the cobwebbed ladder against the gable wall and held tightly to the sides, footing it one step at a time to the overhang. The tea-saucer eyes blinked, taking me in quite deliberately. I brushed feathers with one hand, the other gripping the eave. Soft as softness ever could be. Not wanting to suffocate the owl, I wrapped a tea towel about it, exposing the head. Beak swift deliverer of a blow, I recoiled and withdrew my hand. Perhaps, teetering on the edge of the garage, I might take flight myself over the treetops? I pushed the feathered body away from the trapping point. It slid towards the eave and I moved to stop its fall. So light it was, so inconsequential. As it fell against my spread arm it cast its wings apart and took off for the now appearing moon. As I reached solid ground and folded the ladder against the wall a dark shadow barreled close to my head, rippling my hair in the passing. A spasm of pain ricked my side as the truth of imprisoned life struck me as the only lot I'd ever know.

A Bum-note Baritone

Our bathroom was not much bigger than the average sized coffin. A small sink, even smaller bath, and a toilet with a wooden seat, and we fought like savages to take our turn inside its narrow walls. My father was a man concerned with appearances; whether it was the wearing of a shirt and tie to work each day, or the sharp crease in the pants my mother ironed for him each week. She did the laundry, cigarette dangling from her lip, the smoke forming a cloud up by the ceiling in our sitting room as she watched Agatha Christie mysteries on the television. Proper on the outside, he concerned himself with satisfying how other people viewed him, whether it was the parish priest, or the old woman who ran the small newsagents across the road from our house. Inside the house, his guard lowered, he passed gas at the dinner table, driving my mother wild with rage, oblivious to her genteel ways. Probably the fact he worked away from home for most of their marriage led to the state of their union being tolerable. He clicked his Rosary beads like my mother's knitting needles, counting out mysteries; sorrowful, glorious, joyful. In the close quarters of the bathroom he sang bum baritone notes and combed Brylcreem into his neatly cut hair. Quite a figure he cut in his Jockey y-fronts, Johnson's talcum powder billowing everywhere, the old-fashioned bottle of Old Spice shaken and slapped on both palms and then both cheeks. Today I scour the earth for his scent, the folds of his jowls where sweat and aftershave coalesced. He is lost to me, much the same as he was lost to me when he was alive. My finger traces dust in my mother's bedroom, and I imagine his dead cells still there, fragments of his essence trapped in a house he never cared for a jot. It matters not that my childhood was edged with the faint color of sadness, the fluid memories of long-ago arguments and Richter scale door slams a blurry line across the blank page.

Old-Fashioned Radio Dial

Rathgar.

Dublin.

November 1983.

Creosote clouds over the Dublin Mountains.

Red-bricked houses and four boys running rampant, singing, "Armored cars and tanks and guns, came to take away our sons, but every man will stand behind the men behind the wire."

Mam calls order: time for tea, poached eggs and bread-and-butter slices.

Shovel the coal into the scuttle in the rain, next door's cat cries in the dark.

Scratches on the tar-papered garage roof.

More cats.

A chorus.

Mam's ashtray consigned to the rubbish bin before bed.

Sparks hit the fireguard in the sitting room.

Hilversum. Athlone. Amsterdam: stations on the wireless dial.

The neighbor mounts his ladder to adjust the television aerial.

Toothpaste, prayers, bedtime.

The bedroom saints, St. Martin de Porres and Francis of Assisi stand guard on the chest of drawers in the bedroom.

Say the words by heart—*O angel of God, my guardian dear; to whom God's love commits me here*....

Spoons & Fish

The day the Old Man arrived home from the oil rig, Dublin was engulfed in a rainstorm that lasted three days and four nights. On the last day the drops thumped against the pavement and caused the panes of glass in our windows to tremble. The nests of spring birds clogged the gutters and water fell in great sheets onto the square of green grass in front of our house. Mam and I lit candles and prayed to St. Jude for a cessation of the deluge, but the rain kept falling and the flowerbeds turned to a muddiness I equated with the No Man's Land morass of World War I.

Mam pushed rolled-up bath towels against the sill of the front door in the faint hope of keeping the carpets dry. Finally, the thunderous crash of the rain quieted and the rolling, black clouds paled. Not more than twenty minutes after that, the Old Man's key rattled in the latch and he pushed the door open, shouting "High-ho! I'm home!"

Mam rushed up the narrow hall from the kitchen, her apron whited with flour, and threw her arms about his neck. I watched from the door of the sitting room, book in hand. He kissed her hard on the lips and lifted her clean off the muddied carpet, for he'd not wiped his feet before coming in the door.

My father loved me, but his silver spoons were elevated to a place that I couldn't contend with. In the end, the cutlery went with him to his grave, tucked into the breast pocket of his Kennedy & McSharry tweed jacket. He loved my mother, too. They had a tortured existence, arguing over the morning papers, and the politics and obituaries, and she saw him as a bitter soul bemoaning the sinners walking to their doom in the pubs and bars of the city. "You're a desperate man, altogether," she said often.

His reply, usually through clenched teeth, came back, "Weren't you the right fool to marry me if that's the case?"

For ten years he played his spoons at a *seisiún* a few doors up the road. Sterling silver with someone else's family crest, he kept the cutlery polished in a narrow leather box with a crushed velvet lining.

In Johnny Keily's sitting room he'd perch on a small wooden stool and hitch the leg of his trousers up and wait for the signal from

Bertie Ryan with the roaming eye, who'd raise his fiddle bow and bring it down like a knife cutting into a wedding cake. The whole crew—Ryan on fiddle, Keily on bodhrán, Kelly on tin whistle, and rosacea-stricken Rose Kennedy on vocals—would charge into reels and airs without drawing breath for the entire evening, save for drink.

Keily, a roly-poly fifty-year-old, worked in the civil service in Fisheries & Forestry, and often spent long weeks lost in national forests conducting surveys of this pine tree, or that red squirrel population. His joints were poor, afflicted with rheumatism, and the damp of the land cursed him into an early grave; but not before he gave a lick of the *gideán* to poor Rose Kennedy one night as he drove her home in his Morris Minor. It was an achievement of some measure to carry out the coital act in such confined circumstances, and for a good three months, the mortified Rose gave the *seisiún* a wide berth. By the time she returned, Ryan had a case of galloping pneumonia and was tucked-in to a private hospital bed in the Mater Hospital, from which he'd never return.

When he wasn't celebrating the dearly departed, or making music, he'd take to the road in his Ford Cortina and spend his days fly-fishing at the Boyne River, or the Suck. Once in a while he'd take me, his tackle bearer, good for toting the fishing basket with its flies and spools. These fishing days were numb-inducing; hours spent at the riverbank, usually in marshy undergrowth where the water leaked into my shoes. Clad in thigh-high waders, oblivious to my discomfort, long hours he used to wrist the rod back-and-forth, carefully modulating the cast so as to surprise the poor trout and pike hiding from steely barbs.

The one time he tried to teach me fly-fishing, the frogs were loud in the reeds, and the dragonflies were droning above the water. He placed the rod in my hand and covered it with his two enormous brown paws, twitching my tiny fist back-and-forth, trying to pass on to me the necessary rhythm. After four, five, eight failed casts, the line tangled and useless, he intoned, "You're a dead loss. Here, let me show you how to do it."

I stood in the shallows in my Wellingtons, as he prized the rod from my hand and made the line hiss through the air and drowse its way onto the water far ahead of him. "Come here, now," he said, beckoning for me to wade out a bit towards him. The dark Boyne water rippled, the sun burning the top of my head as he placed the rod back in my hands and told me to hold on to it and not let go, no matter what. Far off, the orange-and-black fly floated on the ripping water, the midges hovering in clouds of shifting black.

What happened next was a blur of movement, but in the moment, time slowed to a slow march. The rod jerked and the reel zipped out line, as whatever beast I'd snagged took off downriver. I reeled in the line, but he told me to let it out again and the fish would eventually tire. Beneath my feet the rocks and mud, above the gathering clouds, thick white cotton-puffs. In my excitement, I stumbled and hit the water, losing the rod. He yelled at me, threatening to beat my behind for stupidity. "The bloody thing is gone now," he said, pulling me out of the muddy suck of the riverbed. However, the rod hadn't traveled far, and was stuck bankside in the fallen branch of an old willow.

"If I want a job done right, I suppose I'd better do it myself," he said, as he left me soaked to the skin, and set off towards the stuck rod. He untangled everything from the clogged branches and set to fixing the line enough so he could reel it in.

As he worked the fish, I stewed. He turned the reel-handle, slowly narrowing the distance between the fish and the rod, every now and then letting it back out, toying with the fish. A smile lit his face as he tired the creature, eventually sweeping its speckled brown body into the net attached to his rubber waders. "There you are, son," he said, crowing. "As fine a brown trout as you'll ever see." He clipped the line back at the bankside, extricating the fly with his thick, sunburned fingers. "This one should have been yours, by rights, but you're not ready for your own fish, yet." In my wet pants and his words ringing in my ears, I let out a sob.

"Are you a man or a mouse?" he asked, thrusting his crumpled handkerchief at me to wipe my tears.

"I'm a man, Dad. I'm a man. I'll do better next time."

And as the sun receded into the early evening, and the clouds tinged pink, he clapped me on the back and said, "Wasn't that a great day, thanks be to God?"

All I could do was sniffle and agree with him. I hoisted the wicker bag on my shoulder and made my way through the wet ground to the bridge where the car was parked.

That evening my mother fried the fish in butter and lemon, and he sucked the head of the trout with relish, wiping his greasy fingers on the good tablecloth.

"You're nothing but a muck-savage, God forgive you," my mother said, banging the dishes into the sink with a clatter.

He pushed back from the table, left his napkin on his plate and took his spoon case from the dresser. "I'm off for some culture," he said, kissing my mother's cheek and winking at me.

As my mother put the fish carcass into the bin I couldn't help but redden at my failure to land the fish earlier that day. In bed a while later, the window open to let in the late summer air, the airs and the reels of the *seisiún* on the breeze and the rhythm of my father's spoons floating in the window drove me into a dream where the spoons transformed into the giant scales of an uncatchable fish.

Choking Back the Tears

We write across distances, from the gray waves of the Irish Sea to the blue-green waters of California's Pacific coastline. More than this we write across the elapsed seconds, minutes, hours, and years of our lives. Only the other day I looked at the sweeping second hand of my watch and thought, how many times in my life has this perfect circle turned its course and marked time's passage? I was mollified to realize that in my life so far the second hand has undergone over 1.4 billion rotations. In that time I've lived on two different continents, been married to two different women, fathered one child, obtained two college degrees and on the way to a third, and fallen in and out of love more times than I can admit.

My patience is wearing thin and in an attempt to escape the clutches of reality I have been writing my story down. Not the whole story, no. Rather, I've been writing down the love story that's followed me around the world, nipping at my heels like a wanton dog. She polluted my life, with her face, the cheerful aspect of her love, the redness of her hair. Father forgive me for I know what I do is wrong. Yes, Wrong. Church. Return to God. Find the truth in circumstances, the mawkish life, the absconded pattern, fleeting, through the dark glassly, ripping the wires. Each step up the path to the altar reminded me of something, the slog of penitents, a drawn out hunger for redemption.

Flight, wings spread, arched back, the sea below, foam bubbling, ancient rocks battered by the salted spray. I'm choking back the tears, alone on the cliff, my heart cold from the pain of her parting words, the spliced ends of an electrical cord holding my pants up. My Chuck Taylors are covered in writing; the musings of her diary, copied in my meticulous hand, the words she hid from me. Aloft on the breeze the seabirds float by unconsciously, their black eyes obsidian pins. I can do this, I can fly, my love! Watch me run to the edge, see the pattern of my sneaker soles in the dirt? See the flecks of spittle from my mouth as I cry to the elements? Shall I jump now, into the air above the water hundreds of feet below? Take my hand and come along with me because you are the one who brought me to this spot. I couldn't have done this without you. Are those ironic words or are they the truth?

Gaelic storms batter the West coast, the flumes of rain stretching across the rocky fields. I am not from this place yet I was born here, conceived in the center, born in the West, driven to the east, banished to the South. My life is a cross, the sign of the cross, the mystical blessing made by the choices of my parents, unbeknownst to them at the time, condemning me to a life outside the church, abandoned: the lost child. Stolen. Water. Ways.

A chittering of insects, the death rattle of a huge moth on the ground, winged cockroaches falling from the sky, the smell of rain, wild dogs running here and there. They bark. My mouth cannot form the syllables, cannot frame the questions, cannot grasp the meanings. Liberty is fleeting, the Tarot card tells otherwise but it's all at the whim of the reader.

Rosary, kneel, mouth the words, swallow the host, drink the weak red wine, pay attention to the priest and his admonishments. Stained glass catches the outside world in an act of betrayal, the slouching aspect of a shameful fool. Were you not aware of the pain your actions would cause, how her thin wrists couldn't put up with the pressure from within? Not exactly blocked but not quite honest enough to tell the man the tone of voice he used was offensive and demeaning. You have a conch shell from the Caribbean. I have nothing. Mourned images of a time without sin, a failed enterprise, dentist, doctor, horse trainer, useless professions, the iconography missing, the walls bare, the boat rocking from side to side. The Piton climbs into an azure sky, a craggy rock, vine-entangled, spiders and insects with bulging eyes and thin limbs staring at the climbing group. Tinfoil about his head meant the waves didn't come through in such a remote spot and when we stared into the night sky, the pitch blackness, we saw the light traveling across the sky, the space station, astronauts suspended in sleep so many miles above us. Challenges came in the swirling winds, the rolling waves, a lone seabird on the rigging. Match the case, feel the drip of water through the ceiling, seals broken, the sloppy workmanship of a failing business.

Nuns took children from the streets, housed them, nursed

them through pregnancy, enslaved them in laundries. Can the sins of the children be washed clean in the waters of Babylon? I know these Sisters of Charity, and the lost causes and mitochondrial DNA that tagged them as vicious brides of chaos. Night was the worst, the teenage girls, pregnant, afraid, abandoned by families wrecked with shame, choking tears back in the dark, their swollen bellies ripe with bastards destined to fill the island from east to west and north to south. Consider the lilies of the valley and think that each of those children would have been a lily, a fragile Easter flower. Missing families, empty wombs where the children slept before sinning, and now they've fallen in sin, their cells are the whitewashed rooms of a nondescript convent on the outskirts of many villages and towns. Complicit in the crime: teachers, nuns, parents, postmistresses, and ordinary people. Guilty as charged.

In blue she'll weave her way through the crowds, the sheen of her hair reflecting the lights from the ceiling, her cheeks flushed from the attention. Who told you that you could write? The notion should have been disabused, drowned like a puppy at birth. Hold it under, wait for the wriggling to cease, the escaping bubbles of air, the gasping of the poor mite trying to hang on to life. With a deliberate stitch she could make all the difference between life and death. We're all prone to dream the solitude of our subconscious. In the dark the feeling is laid back and the hair fans out on the pillow, the piercing blue catches you with a sense of uncertainty, an immediate notion of being caught looking at something you shouldn't be observing. No need. Move along now, approach from another aspect, take a different tack; move the queen's pawn first this time. The result may be the same but there's the chance of a surprise factor at work here and you might end up controlling the center of the board.

Waiting, Softly Crooning

We packed the house up, filling cardboard boxes with her baggage, her stiff mouth frozen in mid-sentence as she came to an abrupt end over dinner a week ago last Tuesday. It was my brother's idea to leave her sitting at the table, the centerpiece of her own finished world. With as gentle a touch as possible we folded her hands on her napkin, the frilled Connemara lace one she'd gotten on her wedding day. She sat adjacent to the bottle of Redbreast, half-consumed, and as the week passed the dust settled on her like the faintest covering of snow.

Neither of us contacted any relatives to report her demise; rather, we answered the phone when it rang and offered news of her condition to whoever was on the other end of the line. My brother stepped down to the local post office with our mammy's pension book and the 'ould wan behind the glass enquired after her, sending along all good wishes, saying, "God, isn't it a pity she can't leave the house any more? But, surely you wouldn't want her wandering off on her own and toppling under the wheels of a bus or a lorry, would you?" The brother relayed her message to the corpse as we divided up the pension in the kitchen, unscrewing the top of the whiskey bottle and pouring a solid measure into his coffee cup.

Through the open door to the dining room we could see her shadow on the wall. In death as in life she would continue to look after the pair of us, at least until we were no longer able to keep up the artifice. In the meantime, I'd drawn the straw for the upkeep of her fleshy face, and with the hand mirror from her dressing table I would hold it out for her to approve of my hairdressing skills. Delicately, not wanting to upset her and land her on the floor, I painted her face twice weekly, monitoring the decay as the lines tightened and her features faded. In my heart of hearts I knew she was dead and gone, but I couldn't let go of the chance she was still in there, watching, waiting, softly crooning her Percy French songs and reciting her favorite lines from "The Playboy of the Western World."

It was the flood that did it for us in the end. A frozen pipe cracked in the village and left us isolated for the better part of a week.

The priest rowed up in a small skiff, his weight lifting the prow dangerously out of the flowing water. As he edged nearer to the window we tried to pull the curtains shut, but the rod gave way and collapsed on the carpet. He got a nasty shock when he saw our mammy's skull grinning out at him from the table. A skull that has desiccated so soon, a skull that once sang lullabies, a skull so white as to blend in with falling snow, a skull whose teeth loosely rattle yellow in their sockets, a skull that kissed young boys' heads at bedtime, that once recited the nightly prayers, a skull that sang hallelujahs in the church nave, a skull beset with pain and suffering and the deception of errant sons.

They came for us when the waters receded. Social workers, undertakers, coroners, police; the real flood. We stayed together after the funeral, after we buried our mammy in the leafy cemetery on the borders of two counties, at last reunited with our father.

The Past of Christmases

The Yule approaches, a full moon obscured by clouds, stars in the night invisible to the prowling coyotes out and about on their rounds. The great horned owls are yet asleep, their orbed eyes shut, shut eyes orbed, shushed in their roosts as traffic plows its way south. Trees like towers, chimneys expel woodsy smoke. White lights are wrapped around the trunk of the neighbor's avocado tree, and the skunk, crossword-colored, reposes on the road. The rats in mourning for their fallen friend, narrow armbands on skinny limbs. My eyes are weighed down by san serif fonts and shocking handwriting, and the kettle hisses whistles on the hob. *O, Come All Ye Faithful* rings about the room, the carolers' chiming voices drawing me back into the past of Christmases in Dublin, the snow an imperative never to exist. Tears. The sadness of twenty years abroad. Lights shine on the tree. The angels roost in pine needles, and the swaddled infant rests in a closed drawer for another few nights. Later, I slide backwards in my dreams, to Dublin's frosty streets with hanging lights and decorated windows. Mechanical animals in Brown Thomas' window nod and bob their furred and feathered heads, whilst down the road in O'Neill's, the holiday pints are raised to toast the Christ-child. I might return to the jewelry shop where I once bought a fine gold bracelet for a long-ago love, or perhaps follow the mute Diceman on his journey from Suffolk Street to Stephen's Green. Somewhere in the night the rooting, pillaging beasts of the orchard wake me from my dream. The moon is clearer, the trees throw shadows and the great horned owls eye sluggish rats, too well fed on rotting avocados to escape their silent swooping descent.

My Mother—Fully Dilated

Rural Ireland.

June 1963.

A crowded bar shrouded in smoke.

Four taps: Guinness, Harp, Smithwicks, Harp.

Several old men wearing tweed coats and soft woolen hats talk politics in a corner.

Rain.

The widest main street in Ireland.

Flooded.

Bedraggled crows on slick pavement.

Street Lights flicker on and off.

Church bells ring for evening Mass.

The suck of mud as cows move to stand under corrugated roofs.

A homeless man tries to light his cigarette in the betting shop doorway.

My father pours a pint of Guinness and sets it to rest on the counter.

Tree-trunks glisten in the light.

In Ballinasloe my mother is fully dilated.

Some nurses adjust hats and check their breast-pocket watches.

The smell of carbolic and disinfectant sickens my mother.

The Bantam Egan prays to Saint Jude for a cure for the DTs.

Delivery room doctor bends over to see the bare patch of my scalp appear.

Patterns of Death

I stride the staggered rows of avocado trees, the dimpled, rat-gnawed fruit suspended as lights from the distant oil rig, the bright green center a glowing filament of cream. The sharp whistle of the red-tailed hawk, circles high above. A spinner on a fishing line flung in widening circles of leaden power, thrumming with sharp-eyed malevolence. In my hand the secateurs; red, plastic-handled, blade dulled by oiled branches and misuse, my imperfect ability to prune a tree, as clear as the dumb rabbit's obvious pattern of death. Later, between the rusted Morris Minor, where black widows shelter their young, my boot crushes a speckled egg fallen from where the nest sits empty between the crook of trunk and branch.

Old Dog for the Hard Road

The pounding of fists on rattly doors. How the frightened souls shrank back, calloused feet bare, the kitchen an only refuge. Hoarse cries of paid men swarm outside. Carts to remove all possessions, skin-and-bone terriers scrape paws on the worn path. For weeks the summons nailed to the door went unopened. Cakes of thin, mealy flour baked on the hearth as infants grubbed on the flagstone floor. Now the poor, now the jobless, now the faithless. No more the muttering of doxologies, no more the promise of hearth and home, no more the possibility of escape. Under shawls and knitted cowls they cup cigarettes in leathered palms, the roar of the East wind comes down the chimney and drowns out the splintering of the door. Panic, the caul of the firstborn burned in the fire, lace napkins bunched into threadbare bags, along with a few faded photographs of the ancestors. The river swells across the town, cold winter water slap against the muddied banks, rowboats tied to wooden stakes. Regretful glances over burdened shoulders as they make their shabby way to the main road, destination unknown: the old dog for the hard road.

Those Gone too Soon

I stole my way into Thoor Ballylee, of the seven-foot thick walls, and up narrow stairs crept in semi-darkness. The poet's ghost in the corner shuffled Tarot cards, swatted a moth from in front of his face, and beckoned me with a come-hither finger. Rain and wind echoed from without, the flickering candle on the table blowing side-to-side. Spread deck on stone floor, the Moon card reversed, the six of Cups, and the Crone, all pointed the way to a place long forgotten. He sent me to the window to pour the wine in glasses thick with dust. In the below Cloon river the tower's image rippled, and the shadow of an owl flitting across the sky towards Gort in the distance. Through the night we turned over cards, drank deep burgundy wine, talked of words and death and those gone too soon. After a while I must have slept, because when I woke the ghost was gone and I made my way down the ancestral stair to the ground floor and out the arched door and along the fields toward Coole Park.

Thrice Words With James Claffey

I have always had a theory that the reason the British have problems when it comes to the Irish is that Irish writers so often do more with the English language than the Brits have. Am I wrong?

I'm sure there's validity to this theory, given Sterne, Joyce, Beckett, Behan, and more recently, Emer McBride, Éilis Ní Dhuíbhne and Mike McCormack are some of the more experimental and of course, Claire Keegan, a marvelous, lyrical voice. Maybe as an English teacher I'm more aware of the highly stylized canonical works of British literature, but I find myself falling back on the old chestnut, "The British gave the Irish their language, but the Irish taught them to use it." I can't speak for other writers, but I love the playful nature of writing, the wordplay, the cadence that sometimes seems to be so "Irish," that it falls into cliche. Maybe the British resent the Irish for their willingness to write outside the lines, or to invert language on its head, but then I think of books like "Lanark," by Alasdair Gray, and see other writers from the islands doing amazing things with words. More recently, I'be enjoyed the work of Sara Baume who's writing is wonderfully experimental, particularly her novel, "Spill, Simmer, Falter, Wither." Here's to the crazy ones and finding new ways of putting the words on paper.

How long have you lived in the US, and what influences here in America do you think have come into your universe, writing influences or cultural?

I've been in the US since 1993. I moved away from Ireland in the spring of that year, a Saturn Return moment of sorts, I suppose. There was definitely the element of jadedness with life and circumstance in the life I was living in Dublin at that time, and I had my Green Card (through a lottery), and I'd had a particularly hard winter for some reason and was ready for a change. As far as influences go, I'm influenced by place and landscape, by the sounds and feelings of the surroundings. Having spent a good deal of time in California, I have to admit it appears far less in my writing than I'd imagined. Places I'm drawn to are the red earth of New Mexico, the gullies and gorges, the Chama River, the red adobe buildings that erupt out of the ground, the manzanitas and the piñon, the charged air of holy places. I also find other places I've lived drift into my writing; the bayous of New Orleans and Baton Rouge, the rocky coastline of Big Sur. Culturally, my wife's rootedness in our area rubs off on me, the avocado trees of her childhood, the secret beaches she's shown me, the names: Jellybowl, Tarpits, Arroyo Paredon, others inhabited by the native Chumash, who made their tomols (small boats) by the water and tarred the hulls with the pitch that seeped from the ground. Writer-wise I've come to love some American writers over my time here; Annie Proulx, Tom McGuane, Mary Oliver, Sam Shepard, to name a few.

You don't have a very big presence on social media. Lessening the distraction or have you come across the usual gaggle of idiots and trolls?

That's right, though not for any other reason than the time maintaining social media and keeping up with everything takes. As a parent, teacher, and writer, my spare time is precious enough and going down the rabbit hole of Facebook and Twitter is a path to nowhere, particularly when it comes to book sales and promotion. Personally, I've found social media results in a zero sum game when it comes to selling books, and the sheer exhaustion of responding to posts and tweets would eat into what little writing time I've got at this stage. That being said, I do keep a Twitter account primarily for my teaching job, and an Instagram for keeping in touch with friends.

What do you teach?

High school English!

Come across any budding writers? I flunked Junior English but... go figure...

You mean writers in the classes I teach? Absolutely. Several in the last year or two have been immensely talented and I can see them being successful writers in the coming years. It's always really encouraging when you see that one kid who suddenly drops a sentence that makes you go, "whoa!"

Looking at your book, *The Heart Crossways*, leads to the inevitable question about a biographical connection to the work. It isn't a memoir, I always assumed, but to what degree does the work rely on realities? And how hard do you lean on the biographical in the rest of your writing?

It's not a memoir, true, but there's definitely a realism to the writing, rooted as it is in the places and spaces of my own childhood and adolescence. The concrete, the specific, the particular shade of wall, or smell of flower, are drawn directly from memory and I hope give the work a realistic grounding. Some of the events the young Brogan experiences are not far from things that happened in my own life, either to me, or anecdotally something I heard happened to someone else over time. Time, memory and events are garbled into a memory soup that creates the fabric of the novel.

As for the rest of my writing, it's leaning less on the purely autobiographical, more on the physical side of things, and many stories take place in locales I've been in, or lived in over the years. I veer away from autobiography in my flash fiction and prose poetry, preferring instead to rely on characters drawn from my imagination, strange, quirky, issue-ridden characters. Right now, I'm working on a series of prose poems called, "How to Dismantle an Atomic Bomb," and there's little to no connection with my life in any autobiographical sense.

No Claffey bomb then? That's sad. Barring that, are there any plans for a second book?

Not sure what sort of bomb might be concealed beneath the surface of some of my writing. Certainly, I've tended to skirt some of the darker places, pushing in on the edges, but not going deep into the space. I'm working on a long fictional narrative about a character called the Bird Mahony, created for Pure Slush's A Year in stories back in 2014. I've about 600 pages to transcribe from notebooks., and then I'll try and find a way into the story buried in there.

It will deserve to be seen, I'm positive.

Thank you, James.

James Claffey

Irishman, James Claffey's work appears in the W.W. Norton Anthologies, *Flash Fiction International and New Micro: Exceptionally Small Fictions,* and in Queen's Ferry Press's anthology, *Best Small Fictions of 2015*. He was a finalist in the *Best Small Fictions of 2016*, and a semi-finalist in 2017. He is the author of the short fiction collection, *Blood a Cold Blue*, from Press 53, and his novel, *The Heart Crossways*, is available from Thrice Publishing.

He is on Twitter @534mu5 and Instagram as jamesclaffeywriter

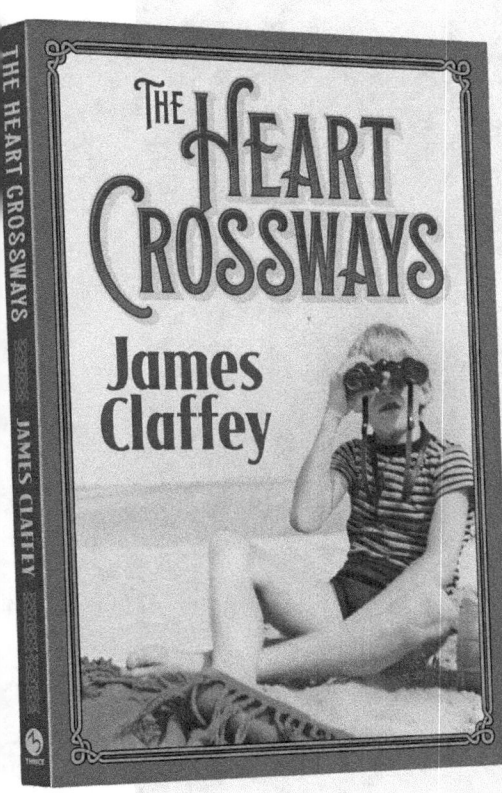

Powder Keg

by Joe Baumann

Before Av'ry took the pill, he asked Jaunt, "And you're sure I'll be okay?"

Jaunt rolled his eyes, the tattoos on his knuckles—one heart, one diamond, a club, a spade; he dealt blackjack at the Riverboat—flashing. "Of course. You think I'd let you take it if you wouldn't?"

"Maybe."

Jaunt poked two fingers into Av'ry's side.

He bit down with his rear molars, breaking the gel cap so it fizzed its contents across his tongue. At first, Av'ry felt only a tingling sensation in his mouth where it dissolved, as if ants were crawling along his gums. He lifted his head from the pillow and glanced down at his body; he flexed his toes and swirled his foot, stretching his ankles. A part of him expected to see something, an electric blue arc shimmering up and down his legs, but his jeans were just his jeans, his t-shirt the same dull gray.

"Relax," Jaunt said. He hadn't shaved in a few days, and his neck was pocked with ingrown hairs. "It'll work faster if you don't move."

Av'ry wished Jaunt would lie down next to him instead of standing like a sentinel; he felt like a prisoner, a patient. He wasn't sick, though Jaunt might laugh and suggest that while he might not have cancer or diabetes, he was, indeed, ill, in need of what the pill could offer.

Finally, Av'ry started to feel it, a tightening all over his body. It began in his fingertips, then moved to his chest and stomach, as though he'd just performed a hundred crunches and his abs were afire with lactic acid. He let out a small noise when his thigh seized up. He clenched his jaw. Jaunt smiled down at him, teeth bright and even.

Av'ry took a deep breath.

And then he exploded.

How to describe being ripped apart entirely, having every cell split from its neighbors, in a way that sounds anything but painful? Because it was not pain he felt. The billions of tiny separations were a rush, a thrill of deconstruction, as if he was dissolving into the bedsheets.

His eyes, becoming nothing, rolled. His mouth watered, lips and teeth and gums and palates all splitting apart. His jettisoned toes curled. He could feel himself turning into nothing. But that wasn't quite right: even if he was exploding, he wasn't becoming nothing. He was becoming billions, trillions, of separate, individual pieces that were invisible to the human eye. How bizarre, he thought, that proximity brought clarity.

Like meeting Jaunt, fucking him for the first time, thinking it would only be the one time. Then having that become two and three and four, and then a one-time thing was suddenly a bigger something. Collected together, those one-times became a story.

Av'ry's body went to dust, every particle that made him who he was splattered across the walls, the bureau, the nightstand, Jaunt's chest. He was part and parcel of everything and nothing.

When Jaunt had suggested Av'ry should try the pill, he'd first said no; he'd never done drugs, which he admitted, voice sheepish. Jaunt sold pot on the weekends to the stoner kids who went to the junior college across the street from their apartment complex. Jaunt had tried coke a few times, whereas Av'ry hadn't so much as ever smoked a cigarette. He took his lung health seriously; his mother had died of COPD.

"You just need something," Jaunt said, looking Av'ry over. "You're getting burnt out."

Av'ry couldn't argue. He'd taken on too much at the law office where he was a new associate, working seventy-plus hours a week to prove himself worthy of partner status, an offer that wouldn't come for years, but the competition would be fierce and forever. He'd joined the firm alongside a trio of up-and-comers fresh out of Wash U, all of them ready to pour themselves into the work. At least one of them had spent four days straight at the office, sleeping under her desk when the senior partners went home, leaving only the janitorial staff to possibly see her curled up in a ball, feet pushed next to her pneumatic desk chair.

"Looks like it's going well," Jaunt said.

Av'ry stared at him. Though his eyes weren't eyes, he could still see. His ears, tiniest flesh carried up to the ceiling, could still hear. Jaunt's breathing was rich and heavy, always, as though he was perpetually recovering from sprints. When they had sex, they were like a lullaby.

Heat ran up and down Av'ry's non-existent body as his cells began being sucked back together. He let out a low moan that came from the whole room.

"I forgot to tell you. The end is the best part." Jaunt slid onto the bed, finally.

What had disintegrated was suddenly coagulating back into familiarity. Av'ry thought his body might feel different, might come back to him a stranger, the ribs and lungs and clavicle twisted with new shape. But no: everything was returning to how it had been.

His lips tingled, the tiny muscles in his face reconstituting themselves. He opened his mouth and said, "Whoa."

Jaunt's breath was close. Av'ry could not move, but he was ready to stroke Jaunt's cheek, his chest, his groin. Jaunt's arms were stretched out, ready to embrace Av'ry as he became himself again.

"Boom," Jaunt said.

Suicide Chez Jeff
by Giorgia Pavlidou

S uicide chez Jeff is sold as a commodity at variable pric-
es. Once in your cart and delivered at the designated
time: an all-smiles, well-trained, well-dressed and well-
groomed euthanasia team will arrive at your door step
to help you exit life any way you prefer. Of course, not all depar-
tures are priced the same way. For instance, last minute sexual favors
are priced according to a creatively crafted menu of erotic options.
A suggested add-on feature to your L'Amazone purchase could also
involve an Ivy-league professor of creative writing to help you draft
a dazzlingly moving suicide note. Rest assured: your loved-ones (if
you have any) *will* cry after reading. For a $4.95 extra, L'Amazone will
guarantee the publication of your last words in its world-renowned
journal of poems sent from the hereafter. ⬤

Kelly Talbot

After the Apocalypse, Day 72

Megan feels the cold bark of the dead oak tree through her pants. In the predawn twilight, a pair of Carolina wrens flits back and forth, carrying pieces of moss and decaying leaves to make their nest. Somewhere in the distance, a male cardinal cheerfully calls out in bold, melodic notes. Her eyes follow the sound to her left, and she spots his crimson blaze in the distance.

She closes her eyes for a long moment and breathes in slowly and deeply. She loves the rich, pungent smell of the soil and vegetation in the city park. She used to come here before, but she'd never taken the time to actually "be" here. Now, she comes every morning. Now, she listens, smells, touches. Now, she is truly here.

She opens her eyes. Thirty feet away, maybe forty, a rusty orange fox paws at something in the dirt. As Megan exhales, she issues a slight raspy sound. The fox glances up and runs off into the foliage.

Megan smiles and stands, facing west. Gradually, the trunks of all the trees warm to a pinkish amber hue. As her shadow stretches far ahead of her, a million wet diamonds burst into brilliance on every green blade reaching skyward from the forest floor.

Mutatis Mutandis

In a haze of umber and indigo, she rises. Across the chasm of these shades, a brilliant white shimmer opens. She glides toward it, her features obscured in ivory starsong. She floats through.

She is feathered by plush fronds as she whispers through them. She hums through copper canyons of dappled amber light. She vibrates between wind-rippled sands and a pristine dome of sapphire, racing toward the distant molten orb on that black line, trembling, gleaming, like a whole note waiting on a dream.

Further, beyond mathematics, beyond science, beyond faith, freed from time, through the ether, through the omniverse, into that which we cannot even know to know, she resonates. I cannot see her. I cannot hear her. Yet I can feel her, there, beginning, becoming, being. Beckoning.

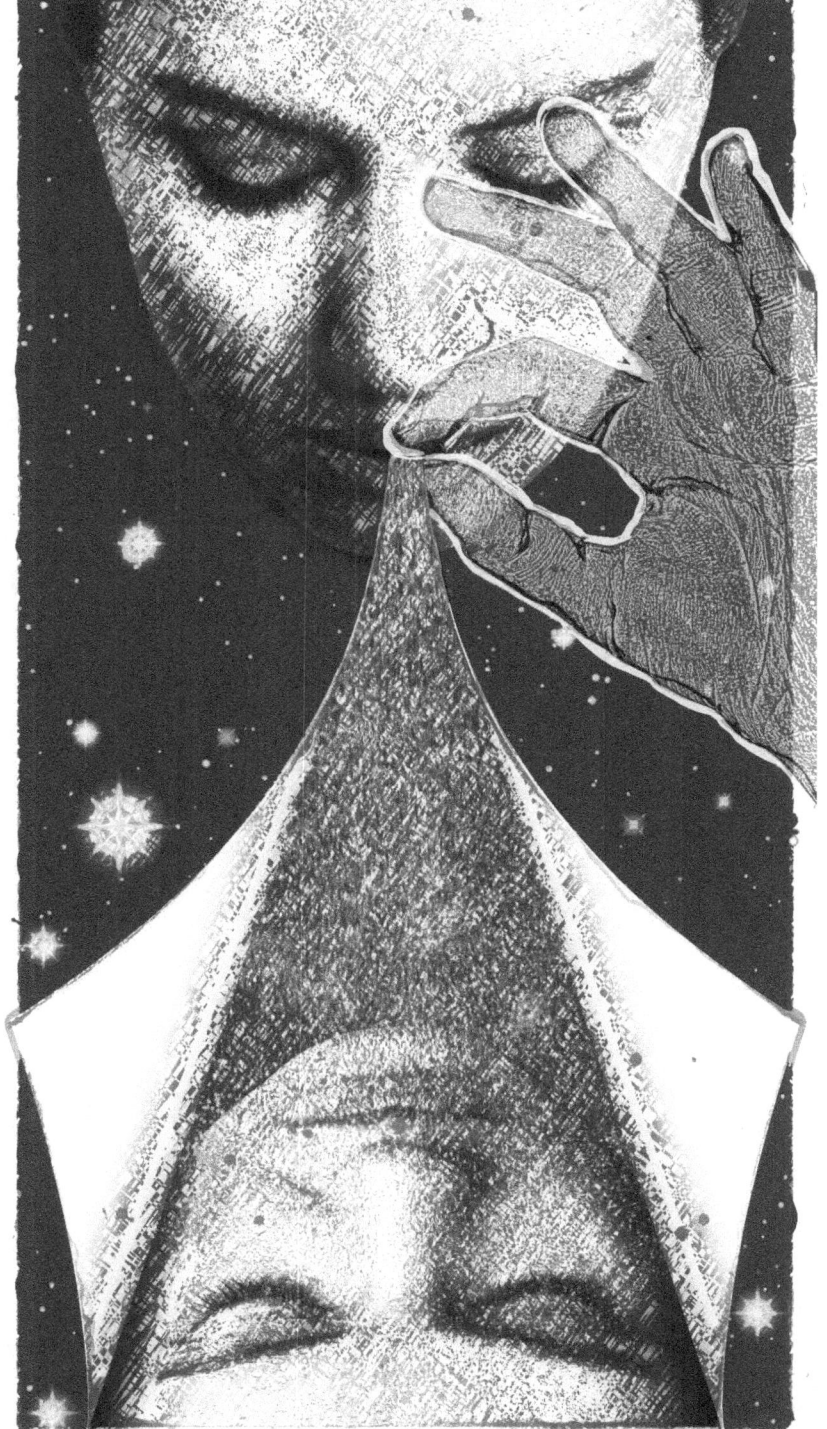

Subject: On Writing Gender-Expansive Stories

by C.R. Foster

Do you know what the word *travesty* means? It means an aberration, a tear in the fabric of life. We use it to mean *disaster*, the flipping of the natural order by an unfortunate series of events. *How is that transphobic, you might think to yourself. Some people will get offended by everything.*

If you look at the roots of the word *travesty*, you can break it down into two phonemes. *Tra-vest*. This word is related to *divest*, which means to take off your clothes, figuratively; *divesting* means shedding your office, or removing yourself from an entanglement, like pulling a loose thread from a scarf. Divestment is a dignified process, even when it hurts. It's respectable. Formal. But swap the first phoneme, and the dressing becomes clownish. It loses its respectability.

The *tra-* in *travesty* comes from the Italian root *trans*, which means "across."

Travesty literally means *cross-dressing*. In the mid-17th century, the word was used to express that someone was "dressed to appear ridiculous." Later, it took on a different meaning, borrowing from the French word *travesti*, "disguised." From an object of indignity to one of scorn and finally unnatural tragedy, the changing meaning of the word *travesty* shows the deep, subliminal disgust and distrust Western culture has for transgender people. I don't use the word *travesty* in my writing. It's transphobic—which is too bad, because it's a great word.

Not much has changed since the 17th century. Think about popular representations of transgender people. We are portrayed as men in dresses. Bathroom creeps. At a reading, one of the audience members asked me "why so many trans people are pedophiles." I've met people who refused to touch me or shake my hand, once they knew my identity. The outright hate and violence I experience are so commonplace that I don't think they're worth describing. I don't blame a single word for that. Even smart people are immersed in their own culture, their own dialect. The codes of our language are as inescapable as oxygen. *I'm not transphobic*, you might say.

Yes, you are. Everyone is. Transphobia is your birthright. The only way to *not* be transphobic is to divest from the language that suggests, explicitly or not, that anyone's gender is unnatural. Or a joke. Or a mistake. You may be essentially good-hearted. But other people who use the same language are not. They hear the word *travesty* enough times and they are convinced that something has to be done to get rid of these unnatural "cross-dressers." They sympathize with Stephen Rea's character in *The Crying Game* who hits his partner and vomits in the sink when she discloses that she's trans. They think of trans people as gross, or as sexual objects. Weirdos. Aliens. Not fully human.

When I talk about gender-expansive writing, I mean looking beyond the obvious, too-easy, stereotypical ways that transgender people are represented. I can tell right away when a writer is phoning it in, or if—like so many people—they've never even talked to someone who's transgender. It's like they're describing baseball on Mars. The fact that these stories are held up to other non-trans people as "great examples" or "moving portrayals" disturbs me.

The truth is, people are surprising. To get to the core of a character, and find the useful information about them that will drive the plot, we need to know more than their labels. The external attributes of the character, or the face they show to the world, is not satisfying. I think that it's tempting to take the easy road, and just avoid all of this stuff. Right? Especially if you're a white, straight, cisgender writer, well-meaning and conflict-averse, the solution seems to be simple: only write about people who are exactly like you. It's tempting to populate your stories with only white characters, or, better yet, raceless, gender-less, sex-less, totally neutral characters.

Staying in your lane isn't the answer, because transgender people are a normal part of life. (Like it or not.) Avoiding diversity equals stories that are boring. It's lazy storytelling. It alienates readers. And most of all, it's dull. Good fiction is an opportunity to grow, always. That begins with the writer, confronting their own preconceived notions, and ends with characters that defy our expectations, prejudices, and assumptions.

People may share an essential humanity, but we have different issues, different starting points, different opportunities, and different struggles. Sophisticated characters contain all of these intersections. If you want to write realistic trans characters, pay attention to us. Listen to what we say, how we say it, and what we really want. It's the same rule as writing outside of your sexual orientation or race. If you don't have firsthand experience, learn from someone who does. When you're in the presence of someone who is different from you, listen to them. Hopefully, that understanding translates to three dimensional humans on the page.

Trans means "across." It is not short for *transformation* or even *transition*. *Trans* indicates the distance we travel from one point of gender expression to another, through the unmarked territory between male and female and all the other colors and shapes our identities take. To me, it's a directive to look past the well-defined borders of the map. The earth is not flat; there are more than two genders. *Trans* tells me to walk toward the wild unknown and aim my compass beyond what I think I know. Past the limits of language—that's where I find the stories worth telling. 🌐

CONTRIBUTORS

Powder Keg
Joe Baumann's
fiction and essays have appeared in *Another Chicago Magazine, Iron Horse Literary Review, Electric Literature, Electric Spec, On Spec, Barrel-house, Zone 3, Hawai'i Review, Eleven Eleven,* and many others. He is the author of *Ivory Children*, published in 2013 by Red Bird Chapbooks. He possesses a PhD in English from the University of Louisiana-Lafayette. He has been nominated for three Pushcart Prizes and was nominated for inclusion in *Best American Short Stories 2016* and was a 2019 Lambda Literary Fellow in Fiction. He can be reached at joebaumann.wordpress.com

Subject: On Writing Gender-Expansive Stories
C. R. Foster
is a queer, nonbinary award-winning writer. Their work appears or is forthcoming in *Black Static, The New York Times, The Washington Post, McSweeney's,* and on NPR. Foster's recent short story collection *Shine of the Ever* was selected by Oprah as one of the best books of the year. Foster lives in Portland, Oregon.

Suicide Chez Jeff
Giorgia Pavlidou
is a painter and writer living in Los Angeles. She holds graduate degrees in Anthropology and in Urdu literature (Lucknow University, India), and received her MFA from MMU Manchester, UK. Both her visual and linguistic work has recently appeared or is forthcoming in places such as *From the Ashes Womxn's Anthology, Beyond Words, Revue de la poésie in Toto, Lotus-Eater, Zoetic Press, Maintant, New Urge Editions, Witchcraft Mag, Puerto del Sol* and *Entropy*. She is an editor of *SULΦUR*, an international and multilingual surrealist magazine.

Kelly Talbot

has been an editor for *Wiley, Macmillan, Oxford, Pearson Education,* and other major publishers. His writing has appeared in dozens of magazines and anthologies. He divides his time between Indianapolis, Indiana, and Timisoara, Romania.

RW Spryszak, *Managing Editor*

has been a part of the alternative scene since the late 1980s. First appearing in altzines such as *The Lost and Found Times, Mallife, Asylum,* and many others. He was editor of *The Fiction Review* in the 1990s. His work continues to be featured in many recent publications, and his novel *Edju,* was published in 2018 and is available from Spuyten Duyvil.

David Simmer II, *Art Director and Lead Artist*

is a graphic designer and world traveler residing in the Pacific Northwest of these United States. Any artistic talent he may have is undoubtedly due to his father making him draw his own pictures to color rather than buying him coloring books during his formative years. He is co-founder and art director of *Thrice Fiction Magazine* and blogs daily at **Blogography.com**

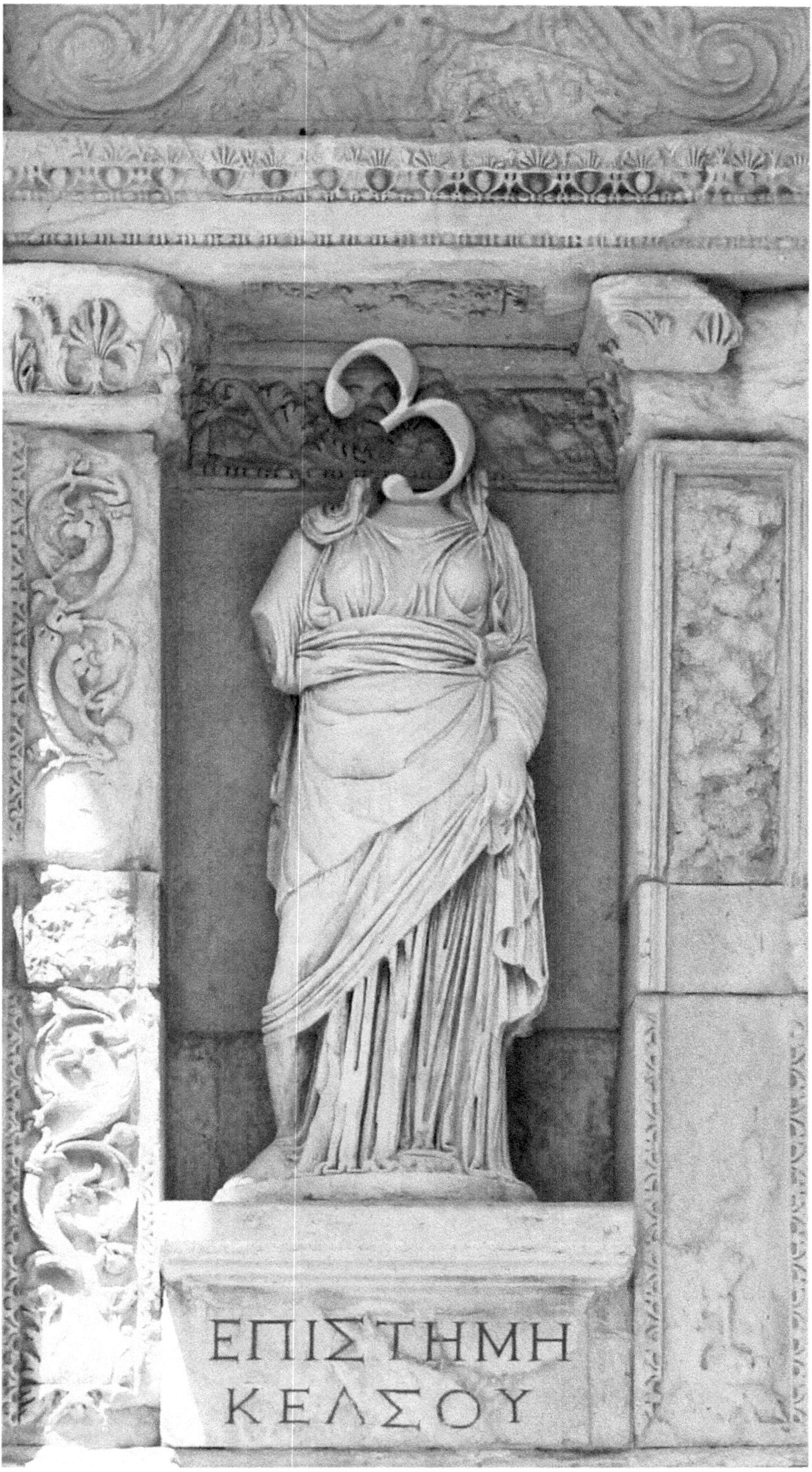
3
ΕΠΙΣΤΗΜΗ
ΚΕΛΣΟΥ

THIS MONTH'S COVER ARTIST

Katelin Kinney

is a commercial photographer specializing in conceptual, product, and lifestyle advertising photography. Currently spending some time in Arizona, her favorite activity is exploring the land and translating that advertising style of photography into the landscapes of the magical southwest environment.

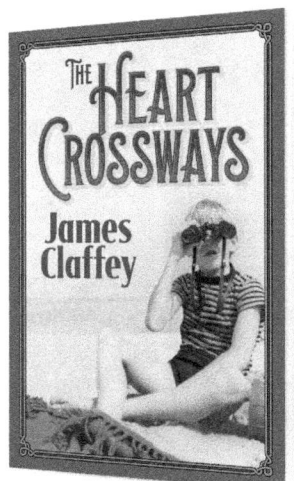

Thrice Fiction

All nine years and twenty-seven issues of our
first volume are available free to download
or read online at **ThriceFiction.com** or buy
in print at **MagCloud.com**

www.ingramcontent.com/pod-product-compliance
Lightning Source LLC
Chambersburg PA
CBHW071234170626

46809CB00008BA/3063